Pudding & Chips

Written by Penny Matthews

Illustrated by Janine Dawson

Floris Books

Five geese lived beside the pond on Annie's farm.

For Gordon — PM

For Rosie, apple of my eye — JD

First published by ABC Books for the
Australian Broadcasting Corporation in 2004

Copyright text © Penny Matthews 2004
Copyright illustrations © Janine Dawson 2004

This edition published in 2005 by Floris Books
15 Harrison Gardens, Edinburgh
www.florisbooks.co.uk

British Library CIP Data available

ISBN 0-86315-496-4

Printed and bound in China

There was Roland, the gander.
There were the girls — Donna, Daisy and Dot.

And there was Pudding.

Pudding was big and white and very, very cranky.
She was as fierce as a tiger and as prickly as barbed wire.
And she was as noisy as a street full of fire engines.

She honked at the chickens.

She honked at Annie's cat, Mickey.

She honked at Blossom the cow.

She even honked at the tractor,
which made much more noise
than she did.

She never honked at Annie, though.
Annie brought her handfuls of grain
to eat. Annie and Pudding understood
each other.

After Pudding, the noisiest animal on Annie's farm
was the sheepdog, Chips.

Chips was Annie's helper. He rounded up the sheep,
and he brought Blossom into the shed to be milked.

Chips loved barking at the other animals and telling them what to do. If the sheep or Blossom didn't need to be rounded up, he rounded up the hens …

or Mickey …

or Roland and the girls.

But when he tried to round up Pudding, there was always a big fight.

Chips barked at Pudding. Pudding honked at Chips.

Chips snapped at Pudding's tail feathers.

Pudding flew at Chips, beating her huge wings.

Pudding always won. *Nobody* told Pudding what to do!

The big white goose was happy living on Annie's farm.

She swam on the pond with Roland and the girls.

She nibbled the lush green grass, and crunched on
fallen apples in the orchard.

Pudding and the girls laid lots of eggs.
Annie found them everywhere —
in the hayshed,

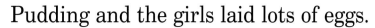

behind the outside toilet,

in the pumpkin patch.

She even found one on the
tractor seat, once.
None of the eggs ever hatched.

Sometimes, when the sun went down, foxes came.
The foxes were wild and lean. They prowled through the
paddocks, dreaming of chicken dinners.

Every night Annie shut the chickens in the hen house. She gave Chips his supper and put him on the chain.

Pudding was left in charge of the geese. "You're as good as a burglar alarm," Annie told her.

The foxes crept through the farm
like shadows in moonlight.
They snuffled around the haybarn.

They sniffed at the door of the
hen house.

They never went near the geese sleeping in the reeds beside the pond. They were too afraid of Pudding.

If Pudding saw a fox, she flapped and honked and honked and flapped until it slunk away.

One warm, windy night a big red fox came creeping through the paddocks. He was old and mean and very, very hungry.

He saw the geese sleeping by the pond, and he licked his mean old lips.

Pudding woke up. *Fox! Fox!* She honked and flapped her wings.

The lights went on in the farmhouse, and Annie came racing outside in her nightie and boots.

But she was too late.
The fox had vanished, and so had Donna.

Two nights later the big red fox came back. Once again he crept up to where the geese were sleeping.

This time Pudding was ready. *Fox!* she honked. *Fox! Fox! Fox!* She flew at the fox, beating him with her wings, and honked until the stars shivered.

Chips woke up and barked.

The rooster started to crow.

Annie raced out of the farmhouse with her jumper on backwards.

But again she was too late.

The fox had vanished, and so had Dot.

After that night, Pudding changed.
When Annie threw her a handful of
grain, she barely pecked at it.

When Chips snapped at her tail
feathers, she simply moved away.

All the honk seemed to have gone out of her.
And then, like Donna and Dot, she just disappeared.

Annie couldn't find her anywhere. She called
and called, but no Pudding honked back at her. Roland
and Daisy swam silently on the pond.

Annie was sad. "Poor old Pudding," she said to Chips.
"I think the fox has got her too. Things will be very quiet
around here now."

Chips missed Donna and Dot,
but most of all he missed Pudding.
He tried to pick a fight with the
rooster, but the rooster ran away.

He tried to round up Mickey, but
Mickey scratched him on the ear.

Every night he kept watch for foxes,
but none came.

Very early one morning, while Annie was milking
Blossom, Chips saw a dark shape slinking up the hill.
He pricked his ears.

At the same time Annie heard a familiar noise.

At first it sounded like a car horn. And then like a trumpet call. And then like a whole orchestra of trumpets.

"Pudding!" shouted Annie.

And Chips was off.

Right at the top of the hill stood the big white goose —
and there, just a step away from her, was the big red fox.

Annie started to run, but Chips was at the top of the
hill before her.

Chips sprang at the fox and snapped at his long
bushy tail.

Pudding flew at the fox's head, beating her huge wings.

Chips barked and barked and barked.
Pudding honked and honked and honked.
Together they honked and barked and barked and
honked until the sun rose in a flood of golden light.

The fox streaked away until all they could see of him was a tiny red dot.

In the sudden silence Annie heard another sound — a soft, piping sound.

Half hidden in the long grass were two — no, *three* balls of soft grey fluff with tiny black beaks and skinny black legs.

"Oh!" said Annie.

Pudding stood up tall and flapped her wings. She honked a long, loud song of triumph.

Chips wagged his tail. And then he rounded up
Pudding and her babies and brought them home.